The Wild adventures of Brad the billionaire Playboy

Episode I - the perfect plan

By

Fred Morales (Alfredo Morales)

Preface

This book is inspired by my amazing family and friends who have been there when I was down and out

It is about a strong bond between friends that are there for each other through all things. It will hopefully make you laugh if nothing else. This is the first volume of others to come, with action adventure and a little romance. What would you do if you became a billionaire?

I wanna thank you for choosing this book, I hope you enjoy it. I hope you tell your friends, and I hope you will continue to follow the adventures of Brad, but mostly, I just appreciate you and hope you become a fan.

Just a bit of insight, there are things in each book that are true and have happened to me in these books, your job is to figure out what they are. And I do love my yoohoo lol....

Acknowledgement

First i want to acknowledge my sister Cyndi who has helped fund this project she has also let me stay on her couch and put up with me while i struggled looking for a job, my family who has supported me on writing this book, my great aunt June who inspired me to write again, and my friends from fulgums bar who was my inspiration for the bond and friendship, most of all God who one night started playing this story in my head like a movie for two days until i finally opened my laptop and started writing, with him nothing is possible, And last to my church family for always keeping me in their prayers.

Through God anything is possible.

Dedication

I have to really dedicate this book to my stepfather, who passed away a year ago, before this book was even a thought. The man who taught me everything I know about hard work and pushing myself to do anything. He was always my hero and will forever remain my inspiration. Thanks, Charlies Lee Hendrickson (DAD).

Brad stood in his kitchen, the wind blowing and rain lightly tapping the windows of his house. The refrigerator light brightened the dark room as Brad opened the door. He bent down, moving things around. *"Ahh,"* he said out loud, *"found you!"* as he grabbed the last Yoo-hoo. He flipped it upside down and shook it, but just as he went to open the top, there was a knock at the door. He looked at his Yoo-hoo, took a breath, and set it on the counter. *"Saved by the bell,"* he said with a laugh, glancing at his nice, cold Yoo-hoo. Another knock came. *"I'm coming!"* he yelled as he walked to the door. Opening it, he saw John standing there. *"Hey, what's up, John?"* Brad said, shaking his hand.

"Not much, man," John replied as he stepped through the doorway. *"I got a call from the girls. They need us to come out there."*

"Everything straight?" Brad asked as they walked through the living room into the kitchen.

"Yeah, everything's fine. They just had too much to drink, I guess," John replied, throwing his hands up.

Brad laughed. *"Okay, let me get a shirt."* He walked into his room and grabbed a shirt. As he came out, he saw John about to open his last Yoo-hoo. Before he could get the words out—*"Hey, that's my last one!"*—John chugged it down. Brad shook his head. *"That's cold, man. That was my last one. You owe me a Yoo-hoo, fucker."* They both laughed as they walked out the door.

"We'll take the Escalade; it's already in the driveway," Brad said as they descended the spiral staircase. They reached the Escalade, and Brad looked down. *"Damn, I forgot the bike trailer is hooked up. Fuck it, it'll be okay,"* he said as they got in. Brad started the car, and they both jumped as loud music blared from the speakers. Brad quickly turned it down, looked at John, and laughed. *"Oops, forgot to turn it down before I got out earlier, I guess,"* he said with a smile.

They pulled out onto the road, headed to the club, the rain still light but present, hitting the Escalade ESV-V's perfectly waxed paint. The black surface gleamed under the moonlight, the rain reflecting off it. John's phone rang, and Brad quickly turned down the radio as John answered. *"Hey, Daniela, yeah, I'm with Brad now. We're on the way,"* he said over the phone. *"Okay, I'll put you on speaker."*

Daniela's voice came through. *"Why didn't you answer your phone, babe? I've been calling!"*

Brad grabbed his phone, glancing at it. *"Damn, the ringer's off, boo. I'm sorry, I didn't know,"* he replied.

She laughed. *"It's okay. You're on the way now; that's what matters."*

"Yeah, like twenty minutes, we'll be there," Brad responded.

"Okay, babe, see you soon," Daniela said before hanging up.

John looked at Brad. *"Twenty minutes? We're less than fifteen minutes away."*

Brad glanced at him. *"Yeah, we're stopping at the store. You owe me a Yoo-hoo, fool."*

John started laughing. *"I got you."*

Brad turned on his blinker to switch lanes as the store approached on the right. Just as he began to merge, a white Mustang sped up beside him, nearly hitting them. *"What the fuck!"* John yelled.

"Fucking asshole!" Brad shouted, then said, *"I got this."* He stepped on the gas, racing up to the Mustang and blinding them with his high beams. Out of nowhere, the passenger started shooting at them. Brad eased back slightly, but the shooting continued. A bullet hit the passenger-side mirror, shattering it but leaving it dangling by its wires. *"This motherfucker!"* Brad shouted, slamming on the gas and

clipping the rear end of the Mustang. *"That oughta chill him out,"* he said in a calm, satisfied tone.

Then more bullets flew. *"Guess not,"* John replied. *"But I got something for him."* He pulled out his Glock 9 and started shooting back. The Mustang swerved side to side. John fired one more shot, hitting the back window. The Mustang slammed on its brakes, and Brad sped past, glancing at the occupants through the window. He checked his rearview mirror. *"Looks like they gave up,"* he said, seeing the Mustang's lights stationary in the distance.

"Well, we passed the store, too. So much for your Yoo-hoo," John said, laughing.

Brad smacked him in the chest. *"Ass."* He handed John a knife. *"Cut off the mirror before it scratches the paint."* He added, *"Look, don't say shit to the girls. We don't need them freaking out. Besides, you know it'll be my fault somehow."* He smiled.

They pulled off at their exit and saw car lights behind them. Brad glanced back. *"Here we go again."* They reached a stop sign, took a breath, and made a right. Brad looked back. *"They're turning left. It's not them,"* he said to John.

They arrived at the club. *"Well, we made it here in one piece, no thanks to you,"* John smirked as they pulled into Brad's VIP parking spot.

"Hey, John, remember, not a word," Brad said.

"Shit, I don't want her killing me after she kills you, man," John replied, smacking Brad on the back.

As they approached the front door, the doorman, Joe, greeted them. *"Hey, Mr. Brad, how are you?"*

"I'm okay, Joe. How's business tonight?"

"Things are great, actually," Joe responded, glancing at his counter. *"We've had 175 people in tonight."*

"That's great, Joe. Keep up the good work," Brad said, handing him a twenty-dollar bill.

As they walked through the doors, a sea of people danced on the floor, girls twirled on poles, and the bar was crowded. *"Life is definitely good here,"* John said, looking at Brad as they approached the bar.

"That it definitely is, man, but I wish I knew why those fuckers in the Mustang were shooting at us," Brad replied.

"Man, probably because they felt like you almost hit them. Let's move on," John said.

Brad looked at him, throwing his hands in the air. *"Oh, so you're blaming me too?"*

"Hey, what are you guys drinking?" the beautiful blonde bartender asked from behind the bar.

"Two Coronas with lime, baby girl," John replied.

"Everyone's up there waiting for you," she said, handing them their beers.

Brad led the way through the crowd and up the stairs to the VIP section. He looked up to see Daniela, Stephany, and Carlie dancing, while Troy, Jamie, and Sam sat at the table.

"Baby, you made it!" Daniela yelled, running to Brad and jumping into his arms.

Stephany ran to John. *"What are you guys doing here?"* she asked, hugging and kissing him.

"Daniela called, said you girls were drunk and needed us, so here we are," John replied.

"She must have missed him, I guess. She spent all night talking about him. I was ready to push her off the balcony," Stephany said, laughing with an evil grin.

Everyone danced as the club's music pulsed through the speakers. Brad glanced down at the bar and noticed two guys—one short and stocky, the other tall and lanky—in suits, looking up at them. *"Yo, John, those guys at the bar look familiar?"* he asked.

John looked down. *"No fucking way, that's them."*

Brad grabbed John's shoulder and whispered, *"Look, I'm going to walk down there. They couldn't have gotten their guns past security and the metal detector, so I'm just going to see what I can find out. Keep your eyes on me, bro."*

John nodded and dapped Brad up. Brad told Daniela, *"I'll be right back. I'm going to check on some things in the office while I'm here."* He kissed her and walked down the stairs, taking a seat next to the guys.

"Hey, I'm Brad, the owner of this place. How are you guys? Enjoying the place?"

The short, stocky guy looked at Brad. *"Yes, we are. We're just wondering how we get one of those VIP sections up there. We're looking for a place to have a night out with our friends."*

"Give the bartender your information, and I'll happily accommodate you," Brad said.

He got up, said, *"Nice to meet you,"* shook their hands, and walked to the office. He shut the door, turned on the monitors, and sat in the chair. The screens displayed the bar and parking lot. Brad scanned the lot carefully until he spotted a white Mustang. *"It can't be,"* he said to himself. He got up, walked to the door leading outside, and ran to the spot he'd seen on the camera. There, in plain sight, was the white Mustang with the shattered back window. *"Motherfucker!"* Brad yelled.

He looked up and saw Troy walking out of the club. *"Yo, Troy, come here!"* Brad shouted.

Troy ran over. Brad told him to keep a lookout so he could get into the car. He tried the doors, but they were locked. Troy suggested climbing through the broken window. Brad carefully climbed in and opened the front door. *"Search the car for guns,"* Brad told Troy.

Troy checked the passenger side and found a gun under the seat. Brad instructed him to unload it and put it back. They searched the rest of the car and found a box of ammo in the glovebox. Brad grabbed it, and as he went to close the door, he saw a glint from the light. Reaching down, he found another handgun tucked away. He removed all the ammo, closed the door, and told Troy, *"Meet me back in the club, but don't mention any of this to anyone."*

Brad picks up the phone and makes a call *"Hey, Drew, I hate to bother you and Jan. I know it's late, but I need you to come to the club ASAP and call Justin too. Get him up; I need him too."*

"What's going on?" Drew asked as he tried to calm Jan down, telling her to chill out.

Brad filled him in on everything that had happened and hung up. He walked back out to the club, passed the two guys, smiled, and said, *"Have a great night."* He went up the stairs, grabbed John and Troy, told them what was going on, and came up with a plan. A few minutes later, Andrew and Justin showed up at the club and joined the group in the VIP section. Brad laid out the plan. *"As soon as they call last call, Andrew, Justin, and Troy, you guys leave. Go sit in your cars and wait for me and John to leave. As soon as you see those two following us, get behind them—not too close, but close enough you can get to us fast. Me and John will pull into that gas station up the road, in the back where it's a bit dark."*

As the night went on, everyone was having fun, the guys waiting for the cue. Around four in the morning, the DJ announced last call over the mic. The guys put their plan into action. Brad stopped the girls. *"We should all go up to the penthouse. We can stay there and keep the party going."*

Daniela agreed, and the girls ran down to the bar to grab some bottles to celebrate. Brad pulled Daniela aside. *"Me and the guys will be back in a bit. We have to make a run to the store."* She leaned over, kissed him, slapped his ass, and said, *"Hurry back."*

Brad and John headed out and got into the Escalade, watching the door for the two guys. As soon as they walked out, Brad started the car. The two men walked to their Mustang, and Justin, parked right behind them, ducked down as they approached. Brad pulled out of the parking lot and took a left. The two men pulled out right behind them, followed by Troy, with Justin and Andrew right behind him. In the Escalade, John looked at Brad. *"Why are we doing this at the store, by the way?"*

Brad glanced at him. *"You owe me a Yoo-hoo, fucker."* They both laughed, and John smacked himself in the head.

As they approached the store, Brad put on his right blinker and noticed the Mustang's blinker go on as well. *"Here we go,"* Brad said to John. They pulled into the far side of the store, and Brad and John hopped out. The two guys pulled in front of them, jumped out with guns in hand, and shouted, *"Don't move!"*

Brad and John stopped in their tracks. *"Hey, guys, this isn't how you get your VIP sections at the club,"* Brad said, laughing.

"This isn't a joke," the tall, skinny guy snapped. *"Turn around and walk back that way."*

"I think not," Brad said, laughing again. Just then, two cars pulled up. Troy, Justin, and Andrew jumped out. The two guys tried to shoot, not realizing their guns were unloaded. Everyone started laughing. John opened the trailer door, and Brad said, *"Get in. And don't hurt my bikes, either."*

Brad told Troy, *"Take the Mustang. Everyone, meet back at the club."* John opened the Escalade's door. Brad looked at him. *"What do you think you're doing?"*

John gave him a confused look. *"Go get my Yoo-hoo, fool,"* Brad said. John ran into the store, grabbed a Yoo-hoo, and handed it to Brad. Brad shook it up, popped the top, chugged it down, and said, *"Now my night is complete."* He smiled.

They got back to the club. Brad told Justin and Andrew, *"Unload the bikes, take them home, and meet back here tomorrow around one."* John asked, *"What are we going to do with these two guys?"*

"Well, first, let's see if we can get them to tell us anything, " Brad replied. He and John tried aggressively to get information from the two guys but had no luck. After twenty minutes of beating on them with no results, Brad said, *"Look, we can back the trailer into the garage tonight. No one will hear them, and we'll figure it out tomorrow. "* They did just that. Brad threw two bottles of water and a five-gallon bucket into the trailer. *"Don't piss or shit on my floor, or you won't be walking out of there in the morning, "* he said as he closed and locked the door.

The guys walked up to the penthouse. Brad, John, and Troy entered to find the girls sitting in the living room, watching *Magic Mike*. *"What the fuck is this? "* Brad yelled.

The girls all shushed him at the same time. *"Channing Tatum is doing his dance. Don't interrupt that!"* Carlie yelled.

Brad threw his head back, took a deep breath, and said, *"I got this. "* He started slowly dancing, taking off his shirt. John shook his head, headed to the fridge, and grabbed a beer. Daniela and Carlie looked over at Brad being a fool. Daniela noticed Carlie watching Brad with a shine in her eyes. Daniela jumped up, ran to Brad, grabbed his hands, and said, *"Let's go to bed, baby. "*

Brad told everyone, *"Find a room. There's blankets in the closet. We'll see you in the morning."* Brad and Daniela headed to bed. She jumped on the bed. *"Now dance for me, baby,"* she said, waving his shirt around her head. Brad stood on the bed, slowly taking off the rest of his clothes. He leaned over, pulled off her shirt, and started kissing her. She took off her bra, and Brad leaned in, kissing her. He threw the blankets on the floor, pulled off her pants and panties, and kissed her thighs down to her legs. Outside, the sun began to break through, birds chirping. Brad's head was buried deep between her legs. She grabbed his head, pulled him up, and he looked at her, the sun glaring off her deep blue eyes, sweat dripping off her face. *"Take me now, baby,"* she said, grabbing his waist and pulling him closer.

Brad woke up and looked at the time. *"Fuck, it's noon already."* He jumped up and walked to the bathroom. As he came out, Daniela's phone rang. She grabbed it. Brad asked, *"Do you want to do anything today?"* as he got dressed.

"No, I'm getting up now," she said to the person on the phone. *"Babe, my friend wants to go shopping. Is that okay?"* she asked Brad.

"That's fine, boo, but around five-thirty, I'm planning a dinner on the yacht, so don't be late," he replied. He went

over, kissed her, and she said, *"I'll be ready in thirty minutes,"* to the person on the phone as Brad walked out.

In the kitchen, Brad looked at the living room and saw Carlie folding her blanket. He reached into the fridge, pulled out a Yoo-hoo, turned it upside down, gave it a good shake, and asked, *"What's your plans today?"* as he drank it.

"Just gotta find a ride home. I got plans today," Carlie replied.

"I'll drop you off. I'm headed out now," Brad said as he walked to the living room. She smiled and accepted the ride. Daniela walked out of the bedroom as they headed toward the door. Brad looked back. *"I'm giving Carlie a ride home, babe. I'll see you tonight,"* he said as they walked out.

They jumped into the Escalade and headed to Carlie's house. They didn't talk much, just listened to music. When they pulled up, Brad smiled and said, *"Have a great day."* She waved as he drove off.

Brad was heading home when he got a call from the bartender at Gums. *"Brad, there's some guys here asking for you."*

"I'm on my way," he told the bartender. He swung the car around and called Troy, asking him to meet at the gas station

across from Gums. Brad got there first, and Troy pulled up minutes later. Brad told Troy about the guys looking for him. They decided to go in and question them. As they walked into the bar, three guys stood up. *"What is it you want with me?"* Brad asked.

"My boss would like to speak to you," one of the goons replied.

"Okay, let's get this over with, then," Brad said. They followed the men to the Palisade Pizza Inn. Troy looked at Brad. *"This is the Rossi mob family's place."*

"Look, keep your head on a swivel. I'm not sure what they want," Brad said. They tucked their guns into their waists as they walked in. The goons led them to a back table where Angelo "Chubs" Rossi was sitting. Chubs said, *"Have a seat, boys."*

Brad looked around. *"Thanks, but I'll stand. Can you please tell me what all this is about? I haven't had any problems with you, man."*

"Look, Brad, we want in on your club and the bar. We want to sell our drugs in the club. I want to invest in your business," Chubs said.

Brad looked around again. *"With all due respect, Mr. Chubs, I don't want drugs in my club, and I'm doing fine. I don't need your money or any investors."* He noticed five goons with AR-15s surrounding them. *"Look,"* Brad continued, *"you've had your boys shoot at me, try running me off the road. We have two of your guys locked up and stashed away. If we don't get out of here alive, you'll never see them again."*

Troy spoke up. *"Shoot at you? No one was authorized to shoot at you,"* Chubs said.

"Well, they did, and as for getting them back, we need to walk out of here alive," Brad said in a stern voice.

"Look, you guys can go. Tell my boys I said get back here on the double, and keep those pea shooters in your pants as you walk out. But this isn't over. We're going to do business together, watch and see, my boy," Chubs said as they walked to the door.

Brad and Troy drove back to Troy's car. Brad dropped him off, saying, *"I'll call you later,"* and headed back to the club. He called Andrew, telling him, *"Have you and Justin bring the bikes back to the club."* He pulled the trailer out of the garage, opened the door, and said to the two guys, *"Hey, Chubs said get your asses back and leave me be."* He handed them their empty guns and smiled. *"Hope you guys slept well,"* Brad said, laughing. The short goon mumbled under his breath, and they sped off in the Mustang.

From a distance, the roar of motorcycles rumbled down the street. Andrew and Justin pulled up and helped Brad load the bikes as he explained the day's events. After loading the bikes, Andrew said, *"Hey, Brad, I have a great idea. Let's get the guys together and take a ride."*

"That's a great idea. Meet me at my house in about thirty minutes," Brad agreed. They took off, and Brad called John and Troy, telling them to meet at his house for a ride. When he got home, John was already there. Brad opened his four-bay garage doors, revealing his collection of bikes and cars, from classic cars like his dad's Roadrunner to his 2025 McLaren W1, and bikes ranging from a 1975 FLH Electra Glide to old-school bobbers and his prize, the 2025 Kawasaki H2 RR. *"What you riding today?"* John asked as they stared into the massive garage beneath Brad's mansion.

Brad looked at John. *"It's definitely a day to bring out Elvira."* (Elvira was his 2025 H2 RR, its sleek black-and-red color scheme reflecting off the chrome-dipped frame, custom exhaust, and 290-wide rear tire—a modified head-turner.) John smirked. *"Always gotta make an impression, don't you?"*

Brad smiled as he pulled her out. Just then, the massive roar of motorcycles rumbled the ground, tearing down the street. Andrew, Justin, Troy, and Jay pulled up with three other riders behind them. *"We picked up some riders on the way,"* Justin said, pulling off his helmet.

Brad looked at Andrew. *"Where to, kid? This was your idea."*

"I got the perfect spot," Andrew replied. They linked their Bluetooths and ripped down Broadway. *"Hey, head toward the Goat Trail,"* Andrew said over the comms. They tore through town, passing and dodging cars, doing wheelies, endos, stoppies, and splitting traffic all the way to the circle. They stopped in the middle of the road just before the Goat Trail. One of the guys in the back asked, *"What are we waiting for? The traffic's backing up back here."*

"We're waiting for the cars in front of us to get through the Goat Trail," Andrew replied. About five minutes passed with cars honking and people yelling. *"Let's hit it, guys,"* Andrew said excitedly over the comms. They took off, ripping up the mountain, leaning into the curves, all seven bikes flying. As they passed the lookout, they ran up on slow

cars. *"Fuck!"* Brad yelled, downshifting to slow down, bucking up to the car in front of him. *"Fuck this,"* he said, passing the car. *"See you guys on the other side!"* he called out.

"Hey, don't cross the bridge. Take 9D," Andrew said, getting behind Brad. They all reached the other side of the mountain, and Andrew took the lead, guiding them a few more miles. *"Hey, guys, this right coming up is where we're headed,"* Andrew called out. They pulled into a parking lot, and Brad looked around. *"A strip bar? This is where you took us?"* he asked, shaking his head.

"Why haven't you bought a strip club yet, Brad? We know how much you love them," Andrew said.

"I've thought about it, honestly, but I know how pissed Daniela would be, to be honest," Brad answered as they walked in.

Justin opened the door, and a slew of half-dressed women turned to look at the guys across the floor. Through the crowd, they could see the dimly lit stage, where a dancer spun upside down on the pole, her topless body glistening under the poorly lit stage lights, catching Andrew's eye. They took a seat next to the stage. The waitress, in a short, tight leather mini skirt, half-crop shirt, and fishnets, came to take their order. *"Just bring us three pitchers of your best beer on tap and eight glasses,"* Brad told her. She shook her ass at the guys as she left to get their drinks.

"See, that's the shit I'm talking about," John said with excitement, checking out her ass as she walked away.

The dancer from the stage came over and sat next to Andrew. *"Hey, I'm Bambi,"* she said, reaching out her hand to the guys. They introduced themselves. Andrew said, *"Brad, this place is the one you should buy,"* with a nervous laugh.

Bambi looked over. *"Hey, I can make that happen. The owner wants out,"* she said with a shrug.

Brad smiled as a few more dancers came and sat at the table. Troy got up and pulled two tables together so everyone had a place to sit. The girls asked about their bikes and if they'd take them for a ride. *"We all have girlfriends,"* the guys told them. The three new riders offered the girls rides, and they left with three of the dancers. The waitress came back to check on everyone, and Brad ordered a round of Jägerbombs for the table. She returned with the shots and handed Brad a piece of paper. *"Call me,"* she said as she walked off. Brad tossed it on the table.

Bambi got up. *"I'll be right back,"* she said and walked off. The three guys returned from their ride with the girls. Some of the guys went to the stage, throwing money and having a blast. Brad sat at the table, drinking his beer with Andrew, when Bambi returned with an overweight older man. *"This is James. He's the owner of this place,"* she told Brad.

They shook hands, and James sat down. *"So, Brad, Bambi says you're interested in buying this place,"* James said.

Brad chuckled. *"Why are you wanting to sell this place?"*

"Well, honestly, I'm getting older, and I just want to sit on the beach in Bora Bora with Jasmin and enjoy the rest of my days," James explained.

"Oh, Jasmin, your wife?" Brad asked.

"Nah, Jasmin's the girl on stage," James said, smiling with pride.

Brad looked at the stage, where a beautiful redheaded girl was dancing. *"Good for you,"* Brad said with a confused look.

"Yup, that's her dream for us. I just need the extra money and free time," James said.

Andrew leaned over to Brad. *"Please, man, get this place. I'll run it. You won't have to worry about anything, man, I swear I got this."*

Brad, with a look of realization, said, *"This is why you brought us here, ain't it?"*

Andrew smiled and looked at James. *"So, how much were you thinking?"* he asked James.

"Honestly, around two million," James said.

"What's your monthly profit?" Brad asked.

"To be real, about five to six thousand a month, but it has potential for more," James said.

Andrew looked at Brad, hands in a praying position. Brad took a deep breath, exhaled, and said, *"I'll tell you what. One point five million, you let me look at the books first, and you have a deal today. You can start your life with Jasmin."*

James looked at Brad in disbelief. *"Are you for real?"*

Brad extended his hand. *"I am."*

"Deal!" James said excitedly, shaking Brad's hand. *"Next round is on the house for the whole bar!"* he yelled to the bartender.

"We just need to get my lawyer to draw up the papers," Brad said, telling Andrew, *"Get Noah on the phone, and don't take no for an answer. Tell him to get down here ASAP. We need this done today."*

Just then, Brad's phone rang. It was Carlie, crying. *"Brad, I need your help. I need you to come get me, please,"* she said, sniffling.

"Girl, I'm on my bike, an hour away. What's going on?" Brad asked.

"Nothing. If you don't wanna help, I'll find another way," she said in a scared, whining voice.

"No, I just want you to know I'm an hour away. Can you wait?" he asked.

"Yes, I'm good where I am. I'll drop you my location. Thank... thank you so much," she said before hanging up.

Brad looked at Andrew and John. *"You're in charge here. And don't forget the books,"* he yelled as he gathered his things. He walked up to the waitress, handed her a hundred-dollar bill and her phone number back. *"Thanks, you're a beautiful woman, but I have a girlfriend, and looks like I'm gonna be your new boss. Keep up the good work."*

Noah is on the way *"he says you owe him and Bella btw,"* Andrew yells out as Brad is walking out the door. Brad puts Carlie's location in his GPS and takes off, flying down the road whipping through traffic. Just as he gets back over the mountain, he notices a car that seems to be following him, so he speeds up dodging through cars. The car speeds up after Brad, so cuts through traffic shooting down 9. The passenger starts shooting at him as Brad blasts his way around cars, he takes off leaving them in the dust.

"What now," Brad thinks to himself as he clears through the traffic and loses the car. Focused and back on track, he gets to where the GPS says Carlie is at. He takes his helmet off and sees her running from beside the house. She runs up to him, *"let's go,"* she says in a rushing, scared voice. She starts to get on the bike. Brad stops her as he takes off his helmet, *"Tell me what's wrong, girl."*

She sighs, *"Well I went out on a date with this guy, he was real nice, and after we ate, I told him I was ready to go home. We get in his car, he takes me here, says he had to do something real fast so I go in. Then he starts grabbing me, trying to kiss me and feel on me. I told him no, I told him I wanted to go. He said no, so I kicked him in the balls, ran out, and hid behind the house. That's when I called you."*

Brad, by this time, was off his bike and walking to the door. Carlie grabs him by the arm, *"let's just go, this isn't why I called you,"* she said, *"I'm ok, it's ok."*

Brad shakes her off his arm, *"it's not ok, you're not ok,"* he says as he bangs on the door. This tall, lanky goof guy opens the door, *"What the fuck do you want? Get this trash out of my yard,"* he says, yelling at Brad.

"You're trash, man. No means no. Maybe if you were a decent guy you would have gotten a second date. Maybe if you weren't an ass, this great woman over here would have given you a chance," Brad yells at the douchebag.

The guy punches Brad in the eye, Brad swings back hitting him in the jaw then tackles him into the house. The douchebag trying to get up yelling, *"I'm going to kill you, man!"* Brad punches him twice in the mouth, stands up, pulls out his 9mm, cocks it back. Carlie grabs Brad, *"NO!"* she yells out, *"he's not worth it, let's go,"* she yells as she starts to walk out of the door.

Brad puts his gun back, looks down, *"you're lucky she's here but if I ever hear you mistreat another female, I will be back."* They walk back to his bike. *"Put this on,"* Brad says as he hands her his helmet. They take off down the road.

Brad pulls up to the side of Carlie's house. She jumps off, pulls off the helmet and hands it to him. She looks up at his face, *"omg look at your eye,"* she says as she grabs his face, *"I'm so sorry Brad."* He grabs the helmet, looks at her with a smile, *"nah don't be, you're worth it kiddo, as long as you're safe."* Carlie looks at him with a hidden passion, grabs his hand, *"why can't all guys be like you?"* she asks.

Brad just smiles, *"when are you going to actually pick a nice guy?"* he replies. She starts to say something when Brad's phone goes off, *"shit, it's Daniela, fuck our dinner."* He answers the phone, *"hey babe I'm on my way home now to get ready I'll meet you on the yacht."*

Daniela says, *"ok babe I was just calling to let you know I'm running a little late myself but I'll see you shortly."* Brad hangs up, looks at Carlie, *"love you girl but I gotta run."* She kisses him on the cheek softly and slowly lets it linger. Brad pulls back, puts on his helmet, and shoots home. He calls the caterer and florist as he runs in the door and jumps in the shower. He dries off, looking in the closet for what to wear, *"ahh perfect,"* he says to himself pulling out a sleek silk red shirt, black slacks, black dinner jacket, and red and black dress shoes.

He gets dressed, looks at the door mirror, *"damn I look good,"* he says to himself. He then looks up at the ceiling mirror, *"I'd do me,"* he says shrugging his shoulders, then walks out to the garage, pushes the button to open the doors, *"hmmm what to take,"* he thinks as he looks at all his cars. He looks down at his outfit, *"with this it has to be the McLaren w1,"* he says with a smile. His slick midnight black McLaren with hints of red, fully blacked out, plush black and red racing seats—it is a sexy ass car, *"just like me,"* he says as he gets in and spins out down the driveway.

Brad rushes to the marina. *"Great, I beat her here,"* he says as he gets out and walks up to the dock. As the caterers rush to get everything done, he checks on the flowers beautifully arranged out on the deck, *"great job guys thanks so much,"* he calls out to the staff. Just then he hears a car, looks up to see her pearl white BMW 840i pulling up. He rushes to the car, opens the door, reaches his hand down, she takes his hand as he helps her out of the car.

He looks down at her in her black fluffed dress, red stilettos, silk sheer thigh highs, *"damn babe you look great, that dress looks amazing on you."* Daniela smiles, looks up at him, her smile quickly turns to confusion, *"what happened to your eye babe?"* she asks while grabbing his face.

"Nothing boo it's fine, Carlie was caught up in something so I went and handled it, that's all, no biggie."

"No biggie? This isn't a no biggie, look at your fucking eye, and Carlie—why did she call you? Why did you feel you needed to run to her side?"

"Babe stop don't make this a big thing, everyone calls me, you know that, and you know I'm not going anywhere so please stop, let's not ruin the night."

"Yeah I know they do, that's how we got together almost five years ago. You came to fix my flat tire in the middle of the night in a damn suit and tie like a dummy, and that's how I fell in love with you. But you can't go around trying to be everyone's knight in shining armor. But you're right," she says as she takes a deep breath, *"let's enjoy this night, definitely can't take pictures of it tho, thanks for that."* She grabs his hand and they walk down the dock.

Her face lights up as they walk to the plank onto the yacht, *"oh my god, look how beautiful everything is, the flower arrangement is amazing."* Brad looks at her with a smile, *"not as beautiful or amazing as you honey."* Daniela blushes at him. They walk to the table, Brad pulls out her chair and gets her set then sits down. The maître d' brings out the food as the captain blows the whistle and yells, *"shoving off,"* as they leave the docks.

They have a sweet and romantic dinner while floating down the Hudson River. As they get closer to the city and the sun starts to set, the city lights really set the mood. The captain drops the anchor in the perfect spot. Daniela takes a sip of her champagne, looks at Brad, *"you thinking what I'm thinking?"* she asks.

Brad looks at her, jumps up, *"I'll beat you,"* he says laughing as he runs to their quarters stripping as he runs down the stairs. Daniela runs close behind, pulling off her dress and kicking off her shoes. Brad runs to the closet fully naked by this point, grabs his wetsuit. Daniela runs over butt naked, pushes him on the bed on her way to the closet, grabbing her wetsuit. She tries to run past Brad but he grabs her and pulls her on the bed.

He gets up and zips up his suit and runs back up the stairs to the side of the yacht and uncovers the jet skis. Daniela runs up behind him and jumps on the pink jet ski. Brad jumps on the red one and pushes the button to drop them into the water. They both take off towards the Statue of Liberty, crossing between each other laughing and playing. As they approach the statue, they circle around it both in opposite directions, Daniela slightly in the lead.

As they get back to the yacht she throws her hands up, yelling, *"I win, I win,"* with a big smile on her face. Brad comes beside her, splashing a big wave at her, *"yup you win,"* he says laughing as hard as he can watching her wipe the water from her face.

"Sore loser!" she yells out, still smiling. Brad pulls beside her, ties the skis together, jumps behind her, puts his arms around her, kissing the back of her neck, *"come get your prize,"* he says as he unzips her wetsuit and starts pulling it down.

She pushes him back and spins around, grabs him by the arms, looks at him, pulls him closer, *"why do you think you're my prize?"* she asks while kissing him.

"Because you're always my prize," he whispers in her ear.

Brad continues to pull down her suit, the sun setting right behind them, the light of the moon glistening off Daniela's soft skin. As they make love under the moon's light back on the yacht, Brad's phone is ringing off the hook.

Back at John's house, he is pacing the floor, *"where is this fool, hope everything is ok."* Steph grabs his hand, *"Brad is fine, come relax with me on the couch,"* she tells him as she pulls him down to the couch.

Back at the yacht, Brad finishes putting the jet skis back up, Daniela is downstairs drying off, and Brad sees his phone on the table and calls John back as he walks down the stairs.

John answers the phone out of breath, *"hey man you good?"* he asks Brad.

"Yeah I'm fine, are you ok?" Brad asks, *"you're the one out of breath,"* he says laughing.

"I'm great," John replied, *"Steph just finished having her way with me on the couch, that's all."*

"Well I guess I called at the perfect time."

"Yeah perfect, Steph's still sitting here with her tits out drinking water," John says with a smile on his face.

"Wait, her tits are still out right now? Send me a picture right now or it didn't happen."

Daniela throws a pillow at Brad, *"men are pigs,"* she says laughing.

"Oh you want a picture of her tits?" John says out loud.

You can hear Steph in the background, *"you better not,"* as she runs out of the living room laughing.

"Hey let's meet up tonight," John says.

Brad looks at Daniela, *"sure, let's go to Gums."*

They agree, and right before they hang up John tells Brad to check his messages and hangs up the phone. Brad opens his message from John and there in bright lighting is a clear focused picture of John's dick. Brad throws the phone to Daniela, *"that's for you babe."*

She picks up the phone, takes a look, *"hmm not bad,"* she says laughing.

Brad throws the pillow back at her, *"get dressed perv,"* he says, *"head home on the double, capt,"* he calls out as he gets dressed. They head back to port.

After they dock, Brad walks Daniela to her car, opens the door, gives her a kiss, *"meet you at the house babe."* She kisses him back, *"I got a stop to make, I'll see you there."*

Brad shuts the door and she takes off. Brad gets in his car and heads home. Daniela calls Carlie, *"hey Carlie how are you doing after today? Brad told me all about what happened today so I wanted to check on you girl."*

Carlie says she is fine and thanks her.

"Hey look we're all going out tonight, you want me to pick you up? I'm headed your way now?"

Carlie says yes but she's not ready.

"Just grab your clothes, you can get ready at our house, I'll be there in ten minutes," and hangs up the phone.

Back at the house Brad is just getting in the shower. Daniela and Carlie pull up to the house. Carlie looks up at the house. The house is three stories high: the bottom floor is the garage that stored twenty motorcycles, thirty cars, several dirt bikes, four wheelers and jet skis. The second floor, there was a game room, a movie theater, living room, kitchen, two bathrooms, a reptile room and three spare bedrooms.

The third floor was their main house. When you walk in you enter the living room. To the right there is a bathroom, down the hall there's a bedroom that conjoins to the bathroom and another room at the end of the hallway. Standing at the front door it's the living room, kitchen straight ahead. To the left is a huge dining room with a big glass table that seats eight and another little wood table with four chairs. To the right of the kitchen is the master bedroom door, next to it is another full bathroom.

"I love this place and all you have done to it," she tells Daniela as they walk up the winding staircase that leads to the main entrance door on the third floor.

"Aw thanks boo," Daniela replies as she opens the door, *"sounds like Brad is in the shower down the hall so you can use the one over here,"* pointing to the door beside them, *"I'll use the bedroom shower."*

Carlie thanks her and walks in the door. Daniela walks into the bathroom that Brad is in, *"hey babe just wanted you to know I'm home, I'm getting in the shower, I got to get this stink off me."*

"Yeah you do stink," Brad laughs.

"You did it," she says as she walks out of the door. She goes in the bedroom, gets undressed and hops in the shower. Brad gets out of the shower, dries off, and he hears the shower going down the hall so he walks down there, opens the door, walks in, drops his towel, *"hey baby you want round 2 before we leave?"* he asks as he opens the shower door.

To his surprise, there was Carlie naked, soapy and wet. She lets out a soft startled yelp. Brad shocked just stands there for a second with Carlie staring at him. Daniela hears Carlie's yelp and comes busting through the door, *"what's going on in here?"* she yells. Carlie slams the shower door shut. Brad grabs his towel, *"what is she doing here?"* he asks, *"I thought I was walking in on you."*

Daniela storms out of the bathroom, Brad runs out right behind her. They get into the bedroom, *"babe answer me, why is she here?"* Daniela takes a breath, *"I picked her up after what you told me, I figured she needed a night out, and you're right you didn't know she was here. But why were you both just staring?"* she says throwing her hand down.

"Babe we were both in shock not expecting to see each other, we were like deer in headlights, that's all. We are not fighting about this or about her again tonight, please," Brad says in a desperate and apologetic way.

"Ahh you're right," she says, *"just get dressed, I'm ok."*

Brad gets dressed and goes into the kitchen, grabs a beer, takes a swig, *"ahh I needed that after this day,"* he says to himself. He looks over and sees Carlie standing in the hallway, *"I'm sorry, I didn't mean to cause any problems Brad,"* she says in a soft low voice.

"Girl you didn't do shit, everything is fine, come here, you want a drink?" She walks into the kitchen and Brad pours her a glass of wine. They sit at the bar and Carlie looks

up at Brad, *"I just wanted to say—"* she says with a nervous tone.

Just then before she can get the rest of her words out, Daniela opens the door. She walks over, pours a glass of wine, looks at Carlie, *"I know that's not what you're wearing."* Carlie looks down at her outfit.

"No, no, come on I got the perfect outfit for you," Daniela says as they walk in the bedroom.

Brad yells out, *"should I wait, are we taking one car?"*

Daniela, *"yeah we're taking mine, it has more room, and babe can you grab the rest of the bags out of the car please,"* then shuts the door. Brad throws his hands up, *"sure why not,"* he says as he walks out the front door.

Daniela shuffles through the closet, *"this is perfect,"* she says grabbing a sleek red leather mini skirt with matching sleeveless short cut top. The girls get dressed, do their hair and makeup while Brad sits on the couch drinking his beer. He hears the bedroom door open. He looks back and almost spits out his beer when he sees Carlie walk out of the room, *"look at you making that outfit look good,"* he says with a smile.

Carlie spins around, *"you think so?"* she asks.

"You sure do," Daniela says walking out behind her.

Brad jumps up, *"finally we can go."*

"Yes dear, we are ready and sliving," Daniela says.

Brad looks at her, *"so we using Paris Hilton's catch words now?"* he asks as he opens the front door.

"My favorite celebrity," Daniela says as they all walk to the front door. Daniela grabs her phone and makes a call as she closes the door behind her, *"headed to Gums now,"* she says and hangs up the phone.

Brad is at the car with the doors open for the girls. He shuts the doors after they get in and runs to the driver's side, gets in and yells, *"off to Gums we go!"*

As they pull up, Carlie looks at the bar, *"this place definitely looks great since you invested in it Brad."*

"It has come a long way that's for sure, lots of work and money," Daniela added.

"This place has been home for so many locals, I couldn't let it go to shit, it's like a treasure to some people here."

As they pull into the parking lot, it looks like a car show. *"Well looks like everyone is here,"* Brad says as he parks beside Andrew's Z06 Corvette. Brad gets out and opens the doors for the girls. They walk up to the front door. Andrew,

John, and Justin are standing outside next to John's 2005 Porsche Carrera GT talking.

Brad tells the girls to go in, he would be there in a minute. The guys stand there for a bit talking. Justin asks Brad if he would mind listening to a noise his 2025 Cadillac CT5 Sport was making, so they walk over to his car and he starts it up. Brad takes a listen, *"kinda sounds like a heat shield is loose,"* he tells him. They close the hood and walk back to the front door. Brad throws his cigarette down, then they walk in.

The place is packed, music jamming. Brad looks around at everyone there having the best night. Then he jumps on the bar, *"hey everyone I got something to say."* The music turns down.

Brad takes a deep breath, *"look, just over five years ago I used to sit at this bar with most of you, I was struggling, sometimes I couldn't even afford to be here. But you guys, my friends, my family, helped me, supported me, and mostly you cared about me."*

(Everyone silently listening to Brad's every word).

"When I hit the lottery and made my first million just over five years ago, I promised you all I wouldn't forget you. I stayed right here with my friends, I invested in this bar that

brought us all together. When I thrived I def made sure my friends thrived with me. Three months later I made an investment in the stock market that made me a multi-millionaire, some of you joined me in that venture and we thrived even more. The night Daniela called me because she was stuck with a flat tire, I had just gotten back from buying the hotel in Atlantic City. I rushed to her side still in my suit and tie, as I was changing her tire I looked up at her and I fell in love with the way she smiled at me. After that I didn't think life could get any better, I had great friends and family, an amazing woman by my side. Then two years ago I hit over two billion, and here we still are together, and I am still thankful for all of you guys. I just wanna say thanks, and to celebrate I want everyone here to have a great night, drink till you can't stand because no one is driving home tonight. I ordered five town cars that will be posted outside and will take you anywhere you need to. To my girl, our five-year anniversary is just around the corner. For you I want to say there are no words that can express just how I feel, just how much you have brought to my life."

Brad points at Justin who's standing by the jukebox, *"so for you I have this,"* Brad says as he jumps down. (Ja Rule *Put It On Me* starts playing). *"My song to you boo,"* he says while spinning her around, *"drinks on the house for the next hour, drink up!"* Brad yells out.

The bartenders start popping bottles, champagne shoots out everywhere. The next hour everyone is having fun, music blaring, people dancing. Brad and Andrew are standing in the corner talking. Daniela starts to walk up on them when she notices Carlie just staring at Brad. She turns and storms up to Carlie, grabs her by the wrist, *"you come to the bathroom with me now,"* she says as she pulls Carlie towards the door.

Daniela shoves Carlie to the wall in the bathroom, *"do you have a thing for Brad? Tell me now."*

Carlie with a soft scared tone, *"no it's not like that, I mean he is a handsome guy but that's all, he is your man,"* she replies, *"it's not like I am the only one who looks at him, like you—you are so beautiful, guys look at you, guys admire you, doesn't mean they want you or they wanna take you from him. I was just looking, I'm sorry, we are just friends."*

Daniela looks at her, *"so do you want me?"* She asks as she gets closer to her, *"do you think I'm hot?"* she says, Carlie in her face. She puts her finger under Carlie's chin, lifts it up, *"look at me,"* she says as she leans in and kisses her on the mouth. Daniela looks at her, *"I got it,"* she says, *"you're going to help me give Brad the perfect gift girl."*

Daniela grabs Carlie by the hand, runs out of the bathroom with Carlie in tow, runs over to Brad, *"Carlie's not feeling well, I'm taking her home, I will see you soon babe,"* she says kissing Brad goodbye.

"Wait I'll come with you," he yells out.

They stop walking, *"babe just stay here, if you want meet me at the house in thirty minutes."* Carlie with a blank look on her face follows her out the door.

In the car, *"look Carlie don't freak out but I have the perfect plan, we are going to have a threesome tonight."*

Carlie looks at her, eyes wide open in shock, *"a what?"* she yells out.

"Look, it's going to be fine trust me."

They pull up to the house. Carlie looks at Daniela, *"I don't know about this,"* she says.

"Come, get out of the car, it will be fine." They both run upstairs and straight to the bedroom. Daniela opens a dresser drawer, *"let's find you something cute to wear,"* she says as she rummages through the drawer. *"Ahh this is perfect,"* she pulls out a black and white corset, the thinnest pair of thongs

and black silk thigh highs. She hands them to Carlie, *"put these on, we gotta hurry before he gets home."*

Daniela grabs a pink bustier, pink thongs, a garter, and pink thigh-highs. Back at the bar, Brad downs his beer, *"well guys I better bounce before she passes out on me."* He laps the bar giving hugs and daps to everyone. He walks out the door and jumps in a town car.

"To the house," Brad yells out.

The driver turns and looks at Brad.

"Oh yea, you don't know where the house is," he laughs as he gives him the address.

They take off to Brad's. They pull up, Brad leans in and hands the driver a twenty-dollar bill, *"you have a good night and get everyone home safe."* Brad closes the car door, runs up the stairs, opens the door, and sees a line of rose petals and candles leading up to the bedroom. Brad kicks off his J's, starts walking up to the door.

"Read the card on the bar," Daniela yells out from the bedroom.

Brad looks over, picks up the card. It reads: *For the man that has everything, the best thing I can give him for being*

*an amazing partner for the past five years is on the other
side of this door, so come get it baby xoxo.*

Brad puts the card down, he walks into the bedroom and
sees Carlie standing on one side of the bed and Daniela on
the other.

"What's this?" he says, looking at Daniela.

"This is my present to you," she replies, *"this is your
night,"* she says as they both walk up to him, grabbing his
hands and walking him to the bed. He sits on the end of the
bed, Carlie gets behind him, puts her arms around his neck,
rubbing his chest. She pulls off his shirt and runs her nails
down his back. Daniela, kneeled down in front of him,
undoes his belt and pulls off his pants.

Brad stands up, reaches out his hand to Daniela and helps
her up, giving her a big kiss. He turns her around, *"if this is
my night, you two go first,"* he says smiling.

Daniela jumps on the bed with Carlie, she starts kissing
her. Carlie grabs the back of her neck, pulling her head back,
kissing her neck down her chest. Brad turns to the dresser
behind him and grabs the camera that is sitting on top and
starts snapping pictures.

Carlie looks up at him, *"what are you doing?"* she asks.

"Oh this is too good not to capture the moment, don't stop now," he replies.

Carlie looks at him for a second, then goes back to kissing her.

"Don't worry babe, the video cameras are on, they're not missing anything," Daniela replies.

"Video cameras?" Carlie says with a gasp. *"You guys are freaks."*

Daniela pushes her down on the bed, *"oh you have no idea girl,"* she says as she rips off Carlie's corset, her lips softly kissing her down her belly. She rips off Carlie's thong, throwing it to the floor. Carlie lets out a deep groan as Daniela's lips reach her ever so wet clit.

Carlie rolls Daniela over on the bed, *"mhh getting a little aggressive I see, I like it,"* Daniela says as Carlie pulls off Daniela's bra.

"I'm full of surprises," Carlie says as she puts Daniela's legs over her shoulder.

Daniela flips around, now sitting on Carlie's face. She leans back, looks down at Carlie, *"pick your toy sweetie,"* she tells Carlie.

"My what?" Carlie responds.

Daniela leans over, pulls open a drawer on the side of the bed. Carlie looks over and sees a drawer full of sex toys, handcuffs, ball gags, whips, gels, and even rope.

"You two really are freaks," she laughs.

"That we are," Daniela replies as she picks the butterfly out of the drawer.

The room goes black. All you hear is Carlie letting out a loud moan, *"oh my god..."*

The bedroom door opens. Brad walks out to the kitchen, grabs a beer out of the fridge. He walks down to the living room, blowing out the candles that are still lit. He hears the bedroom door squeak, he looks up to see Carlie walking out wrapped in the red satin bed sheet.

"Hey, you ok?" he asks her as he gets up and walks back in the kitchen.

"I'm fine," she said, *"just needed a drink."*

"Wine?" he asks and she nods her head. Brad grabs a glass and pours her a drink.

"Is there really video?" she asks as she takes a sip.

Brad laughs, *"yeah but I'll erase it in the morning if you want."*

"Just promise me no one will ever see it and we're good."

"Oh I promise, they would have to see me too, that ain't a pretty sight," he says laughing.

"So you think?" Carlie says in a whisper.

Just then Daniela walks out, *"a glass of wine is just what I need."* Brad pours her a glass, she takes a long sip, puts the glass down, looks at Carlie.

"Really, after all that you wanna cover up?" she says as she pulls the sheet off of Carlie.

Brad looks over at Carlie smiling, *"here we go,"* he says. Daniela grabs Carlie by the waist, lifts her up onto the bar. Carlie looks over at Brad.

"She ain't done with you yet," he says with a shrug of his shoulders.

"I'm not done with you either," she says to Brad as she bends over and puts her head in Carlie's lap.

"What the hell," Brad says as he walks behind Daniela. *"Round three,"* he says as the room goes black.

Brad wakes up to his phone ringing. He rolls over and picks it up, *"yo what's up?"*

"Hey, I need you to get up and meet us at Gums asap, Chubs and his son are here and they wanna talk."

"Ok tell them to give me thirty minutes and get the guys there too."

They hang up. Brad gets up and gets dressed, he kisses Daniela, *"I'll be back soon, stay in bed, I'll make breakfast when I get home."*

He runs outside, jumps in his 1986 Trans Am, and spins out of the driveway. He pulls up at Gums and runs inside. He is greeted by Andrew, John, and Justin. Chubs, his son, and four goombas are sitting in the back booth. Brad and the guys walk back to where Chubs is sitting.

"Great food you guys have here, definitely worth the trip," Chubs says to Brad.

The goombas get up and Brad sits across from Chubs, *"glad you like the food, now can you tell me what all this is about? I'm tired of your guys chasing me, being shot at for two days. We need to fix this today, Chubs. What can we do?"*

"What do you mean shot at for two days?" he asks, *"I told my boys no more shooting."*

"Well looks like you have a dirty house because I have definitely got shot at again yesterday," Brad replied.

Chubs gives his guys a disgusted look, *"look, the bottom line here is I haven't had any problems with you ever and now this, what is it now that is drawing my attention to you?"* Brad asks.

"Well my son here seems to think your club and this bar could generate a lot of business for us. The hotel/casino in Atlantic City would definitely be a great way to launder money. He tells me he has inside information that a takeover of your assets is imminent."

Brad laughs, *"look Chubs, me and my assets are just fine."*

All of the sudden the front door bursts open. Carlie comes running in beaten and bruised, *"it's a trap!"* she yells out as she falls to the floor. Everyone jumps up and pulls out their guns.

"What's a trap?" Brad asks as he runs over to Carlie and picks her head up.

Daniela then walks through the door, gun in hand, points it at Brad. She looks over at JR, nods her head. JR turns his gun to his dad, *"sorry old man but your time running this family is over."*

Brad stands up in front of Daniela, *"what are you doing?"* he asks.

With an evil look on her face, still pointing the gun at Brad, *"for the past five years I've been with you, five years I've been your girlfriend, five years I've been beside you, behind you, and in those five years you've never seen me as a partner, you've never seen me as an equal, a boss. You lead, I'm supposed to follow. You make decisions, I'm supposed to agree. You buy into this dump, pour money into it, never once asked me. You buy those ridiculous cars, motorcycles, and boats, never ask me? Your friends, you ask your friends, you consult with your friends, you make bosses, hand them business jobs. We take trips, you bring your friends, you don't ask me. Not once did you ask if I wanted to run anything, not once did you ask if it's ok that everyone comes with us, not once did you stop and think, is Daniela going to mind if I buy this? Hell, the way you live, the way you drive your cars, ride your motorcycles, I didn't even expect you to be alive this long. Then I met Jr and we realized we had similar problems. His father was just like you, he had to follow, never lead. He lives in his father's shadow the way I live in yours. So we started spending time together, while you were off playing with your friends, I was off playing with Jr, and so we decided if he kills you I get everything, if I kill his dad he takes over the family. The perfect plan."*

JR shrugs his shoulders, *"sorry pop but this is how it has to be."*

Carlie, with all the strength she could muster, springs up off the floor, smacks the gun out of Daniela's hands. The gun slides across the floor. In the distraction the guys overtake the goombas. Chubs grabs JR's gun. The girls wrestle on the floor trying to get the gun. Carlie kicks her in the face, grabs the gun, sits on top of her, *"really you ungrateful bitch? That man has given you everything, what he had you had, where he went he took you unless you didn't want to go. He might have been off with his friends but you were off spending his money. The lifestyle you lived was because of him, because of the decisions he made. He didn't need to ask you how or what he can spend his money on, the fact that he even included you with his money was enough. And no power? You had all the power. If you told him no about anything that man didn't do it. If you decided you wanted something, you got it. If he was out and you called him, he left, he didn't wait, he didn't hesitate, he came to you. It's people like you that make me sick, you have no idea how good you had it."*

"Look I hate to interrupt this family moment but we have to go, I have a dirty house that needs to be cleaned," Chubs says as he walks his way to the door.

"Yeah looks like we both have some cleaning to do," Brad says, *"so what are you going to do about Jr?"* Brad asks.

"Let's just say he is going to take a trip to the old country where he will learn about respect and family," he replies.

"So we good then?" Brad asked.

"Hey forgetaboutit," Chubs replies.

They get to the door, *"the strip club,"* Andrew hollers out.

Chubs and Brad look back at him, *"come again?"* Chubs says.

"Look, Brad just bought a strip club for me to run. You can invest half a million and be a silent partner. Your goons can have a spot to come, no drugs though, but it's the best way to launder money with no paper connecting to you. It's a win-win."

Brad looks over at Chubs, gives him a shoulder shrug.

Chubs rubs his chin, looks at Andrew, *"you have a deal, I will wire you the money this evening."*

Chubs, Andrew, and Brad shake hands. Chubs pushes Jr as they walk out the door. Brad helps Daniela up.

"I didn't know you felt that way," he says to her, *"and I never meant to make you feel like that. You were the most important part of my life, I would have died for you,"* he tells her.

Carlie puts the gun down on the bar and starts walking towards the door.

"Carlie wait," Brad yells out, running to her. He grabs her hand, *"look, all my life I have chosen the wrong girl. I pick the girls who need me or who need saving, never the ones who want me or love me. But right here, right now, I can change that. Will you be that girl?"*

Carlie looks at him and shakes her head no. She pulls back from him, *"I've been here this whole time, before her, before the money Brad, and now you ask me this? Why now? This isn't fair."*

"Carlie, I'm not saying this is fair to you, not now, but I understand now what kind of love I want, I understand now that it was always supposed to be you."

Carlie looks up at him, *"I'm sorry Brad, I just don't know,"* and she takes off out the door.

Daniela walks up to Brad, *"well at least your whore is gone now, let's go home babe,"* and grabs Brad's hand.

He pulls his hand away, *"whore? That girl has more class, more love, and damn sure more loyalty than a money-hungry whore like yourself will ever have. We are done Daniela, I want you out of my house, out of my life."*

"What about me, I've spent five years with you, what do I get?" she asks sobbing.

"You're right," Brad says, *"I'll tell you what you get— you get the car, the money in your personal account, the money in your pocket, the clothes and jewelry you are wearing, and you get to walk out of here without being in cuffs. Don't go back to the house, don't even attempt to go to the house, I will have you arrested for attempted murder."*

Brad rushes out the door, gets in his car, and races to Carlie's house. He finds her sitting at her doorstep, face in her lap, crying. Brad walks up to her and kneels down in front of her, he holds her head, *"look, if you don't want to be with me I understand, but I don't want to lose a friend. I don't want you mad at me, and I don't want you upset or hurt, and definitely don't want you to hate me."*

She pulls her head up, smacks him on the chest, *"I don't hate you and I don't not want to be with you, I just don't want to be your second choice. I don't want to be your backup, your go-to, I definitely don't want to be your rebound."*

"Ok I get it, I do. I'll just go fuck some hoes and meet you back here in like a week so you won't be the rebound," Brad starts to walk off.

Carlie throws her shoe at him, *"don't be a smart ass right now, I'm really upset."*

Brad turns back around, *"I'm sorry, I was just trying to lighten the mood."*

"I know," she says, *"but I really do love you dummy, I just don't know what to do about this."*

"I'll tell you what to do. You get your ass up, get in your car, follow me home, give it two weeks. If you're happy we get your stuff from here and you move in, if not you come home, we go back to my first option and we keep meeting back here until you are happy. Say you're going to fuck some hoes one more time, I will definitely call Daniela for you."

Brad bends over, puts her shoe back on her foot, laughs, grabs her up by the hand, gives her a big hug, *"come on, let's go."* He walks Carlie to her car.

"Beat you home," she yells out, spinning off, Brad still standing in the road.

Six months later at the opening of Andrew's Dancing (Dames and Slippery Kittens Adult Club), the club is packed with beautiful girls, guys throwing money, loud music. The whole gang is there celebrating the club's remodeled grand opening.

Jay and Sam are at the pool table with Troy, Jamie, Steph, and Jan. Bella is with Noah, helping him in the office go through the books. Nicole and Carlie are at the stage making it rain. There are a few goombas with them throwing hundreds. Back over at the bar, Brad is with Chubs, John, Andrew, and Justin, sitting back drinking shots of whiskey.

"Well Chubs, looks like everything turned out ok," Brad says, leaning back in his chair.

Carlie and Nicole walk over. Nicole grabs Justin's hand, *"Come on handsome, let's go get a dance,"* she says, pulling him off the stool.

The stripper that was on the stage walks up to Carlie, *"Hey, thanks for bringing them up to the stage, it really helped."* She kisses Carlie on the cheek, looks at Brad, *"Hey boss, you two want a private dance?"* she asks.

Brad looks at Carlie, *"Nah, I'm good thanks. I got all the woman I need right here,"* he says with a smile.

Carlie gives him a kiss, *"I want one,"* Carlie says.

Marrisa looks at her, *"Ok boss's boss,"* and takes Carlie by the hand, walking her to the VIP dance lounge.

"Lucky man you are," Chubs says.

Brad smiles, *"Nope, not luck my friend, this is God's plan,"* he says, *"I'm just grateful He's in my life."*

Chubs pats Brad on the back. He then looks at the stage, *"Hey, isn't that your ex up there dancing?"*

"Sure is. She needed a job, we needed dancers. It's a win-win."

They all laugh.

"Well, God always has the perfect plan for us all, we just have to wait," Chubs replies.

THE END... FOR NOW ANYWAY